In Search Of The Hidden Giant

For Michael

A Red Fox Book

Published by Random House Children's Books
20 Vauxhall Bridge Road, London SW1V 2SA

A division of Random House UK Ltd
London Melbourne Sydney Auckland
Johannesburg and agencies throughout the world

Text copyright © 1993 by Jeanne Willis
Illustrations copyright © 1993 by Ruth Brown

1 3 5 7 9 10 8 6 4 2

First published in Great Britain in 1993 by
Andersen Press Limited

Red Fox edition 1995

Printed in Hong Kong

RANDOM HOUSE UK Limited Reg. No. 954009

ISBN 0 09 943281 1

IN SEARCH OF THE HIDDEN GIANT

Written by Jeanne Willis

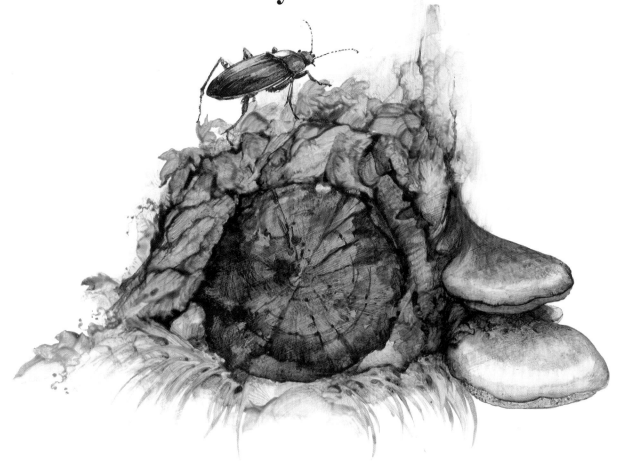

Illustrated by Ruth Brown

Red Fox

The taller that we grow, I think,
The more the world begins to shrink.
So come with me, way back in time,
When bedtime stairs were hard to climb
And my big sister made me look
At giants in a picture book.
I believed her when she said
Her favourite giant wasn't dead
But only sleeping and that we
Should search for him. Did I agree?
Or was I, she suspected, scared?
"What, me?" I scowled as I prepared,
"I'm braver than you think, you know."
"All right," she said, "then, off we go."

Westward to the wood, then East,
We hunted our half-man, half-beast,
A creature of enormous size
With elms for arms and oaks for thighs,
His backbone beech, his hands and knees
The bent and battered boughs of trees.

We crossed two planks that bridged a stream
Whose baked banks turned the rain to steam.
Moist, mossy breath, spice-scented floor,
Strange perfume seeped from every pore.

From velvet hollows, hazy hills,
From musty, musky mushroom gills
It rose like magic, mad and rare
And lingered in the limpish air.
It put the squirrels in a trance,
The butterflies froze in their dance.
Small mounds seemed mountains, twice as steep
As though we stumbled in our sleep.
Without a compass, quite alone
It seemed the very wood had grown,
As if some timewarp had been crossed
And we were stranded in it, lost.

In this torpid state of sloth
We blundered through the undergrowth,
Where thickets huddled, dark and dense
And nettles formed their poisonous fence.
It seemed that every form of life
Was brandishing a stick or knife,
Garotting wire or rope to wind
Around us, or a spike to blind.

We battled on. We were defiant,
Desperate to find the giant.
Maybe we were both too late,
Perhaps the giant had met his fate.

Say, time had passed and day by day
A piece of him was tugged away
By nesting wrens in search of straws
And sticks. The busy squirrels' paws
Had plucked for cones and berries there,
Stag beetles rummaged through his hair.

Red fox cubs' aching milk-teeth gnawed
His fingers and the weevils bored
Until he was reduced to dust.
Should we go home now? Yes we must.
It's getting dark, it's for the best
To leave the mystery to rest.

Yet … what was that unnerving crack?
Is someone there behind my back?
Stand still … I think we'd better check.
OH! Something's breathing down my neck.
Let's walk a little faster, please,
Don't tell me it was just the breeze.
We've woken him! Our noisy boots
Sent shudders down his giant's roots,

And broke his slumber. Stiff and sore
He made the most almighty roar.
No more eerie song was sung
Than his, with scarlet,
    toadstool tongue.

Aren't those his shins now sprouting
    leaves,
Weeds on his arms like scarecrow's
    sleeves?
His shrew-scarred fists? His fungal
    nails?
His ears atwitch with termites' tails?
Oh hurry, hurry, please don't push!
I'm scared of every branch and bush,
Of every noise that's amplified
And not a single place to hide.

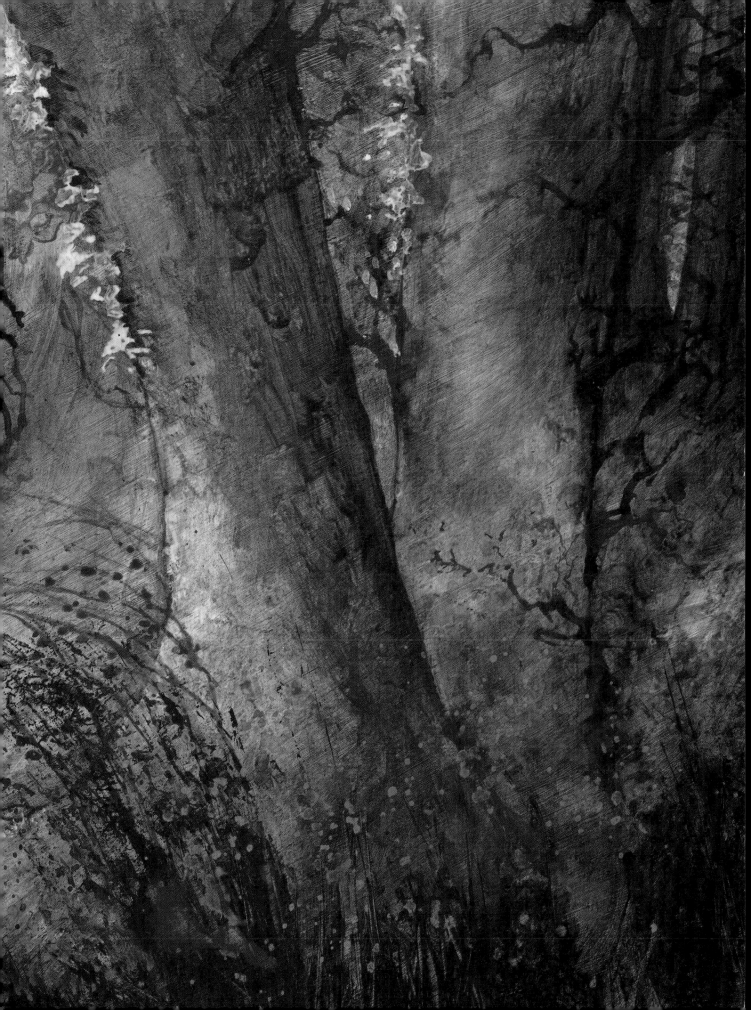

Forgive us if we turned and ran
To where the story first began,
Where dreams were soft and kind and good
And nightmares were not made of wood.
Ah, but say for pity's sake,
The dreadful cry we heard him make
Was really just a friendly call
For he was lonely. That was all.
And being more than just a tree
He yearned for human company.
Is that the truth? Well, who can say?
For thoughts and cowards run away.
The less we see, the more I know
Our giant imaginations grow.

Some bestselling Red Fox picture books